The Moving Mystery

By
Carmen Harris
Illustrated by Lis Toft

ORCHARD BOOKS

The Moving Mystery

ORCHARD BOOKS
96 Leonard Street, London EC2A 4RH
Orchard Books Australia
14 Mars Road, Lane Cove, NSW 2066
ISBN 1 85213 883 1 (hardback)
ISBN 1 86039 097 8 (paperback)
First published in Great Britain 1995
First paperback publication 1996
Text © Carmen Harris 1995
Illustrations © Lis Toft 1995
The right of Carmen Harris to be identified as the author and
Lis Toft as the illustrator of this work has been asserted
by them in accordance with the Copyright, Designs
and Patents Act, 1988.
A CIP catalogue record for this book is available
from the British Library.
Printed in Great Britain by Guernsey Press, C.I.

CONTENTS

CHAPTER ONE

Rat-tat-tat!

Charlie jumped out of bed in his Super Mario pyjamas. Ben was already at the window, wearing the same pyjamas. Ben was Charlie's special friend. They always dressed the same. In fact, they could almost be brothers. Rat-tat-tat!

From six floors up, they watched the man from the Estate Agents bang the last nail into the 'Sold' sign outside the block of flats. Ben kicked the skirting board. He had a habit of kicking things when he wasn't happy.

"At least we'll have a bigger room in the new place," said Charlie.

"Who needs a bigger room?" said Ben stubbornly.

"No more climbing up all those stairs to get to our flat," said Charlie.

"What's wrong with stairs? We have marble races on the stairs," said Ben grumpily.

"We'll have a garden instead of a balcony," said Charlie.

"I like balconies," said Ben. "You get to throw things off balconies."

That was true, thought Charlie. No more of his favourite game, Bombs Away! Dropping bags of flour out of the window, seeing whose would hit the courtyard and explode first. Charlie kicked the skirting board, but forgot he wasn't wearing any shoes. "Ow!" he cried. Ben could kick anything he liked and never hurt himself. But then, Ben was different.

"What are you up to, Charlie?" asked

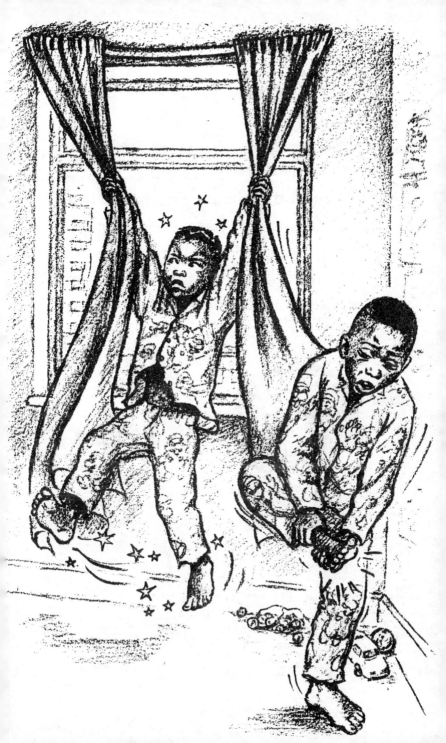

Mum. She stood at the door with a letter in her hand looking cheerful.

"We're not moving. We're staying here!" shouted Ben at the top of his voice. But Mum didn't hear. She never heard Ben. A "figment of Charlie's imagination" is what she called Ben. Cheek!

"Look," she said, waving the letter, "I've just got back from the new house and our neighbours gave me this lovely card."

"Why don't you ever listen to Ben?" asked Charlie.

"Did he say something?" asked Mum, looking around the room and seeing nothing.

"Houses are stupid!" muttered Ben, kicking the chair.

"He doesn't want to leave the flat. He wants to stay here," said Charlie.

11

"What? He doesn't want a nice big house with big rooms, a garden and no more stairs to climb? He can't be very clever," said Mum.

Ben kicked the bottom of the wardrobe.

"You've upset him now," said Charlie.

"Well, you tell Ben that no one's forcing him. He can stay here. It's up to him," said Mum.

Ben was horrified. He opened his mouth and forgot to close it. Stay on his own? Without Charlie! Without his best friend!

"Well, I don't want to move either" said Charlie flatly. "I like my room. I like climbing stairs. And who wants a stupid garden, anyway?"

"Charlie!"

Now Dad stood at the door. He came in and put his arm around Charlie.

"Living in a house you'll be able to get out more. You won't have to spend so much time alone in your room."

"But I'm not alone. I've got Ben," said Charlie.

"You know what I mean," said Dad.

But Charlie didn't.

"In our new neighbourhood you'll make lots of friends — *different* friends," said Mum, looking sneakily around the room. "Maybe Ben *should* stay behind."

Now it was Charlie's turn for his mouth to hang open like a trap door.

"You're not a goldfish," said Dad, closing it for him.

"Mr and Mrs Evans are coming to measure the flat for curtains," said Mum. "They're bringing their grandson, Simon.

14

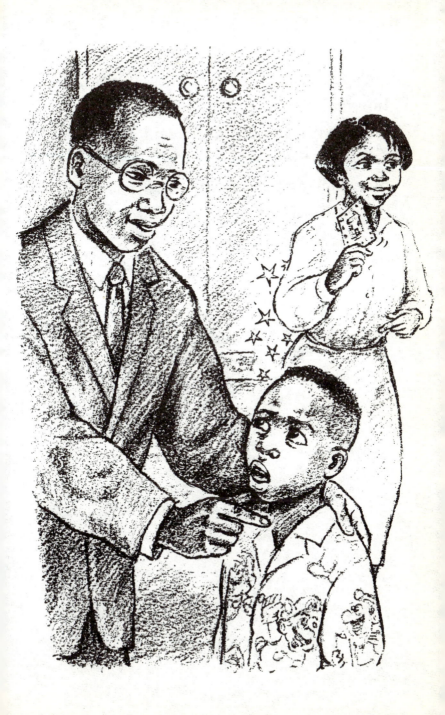

He's only four. Why don't you introduce him to Ben?"

"That's a good idea!" said Dad. "Ben will like that, won't he?" But Ben was busy kicking the leg of the bed.

And as for Charlie. Charlie was already scheming.

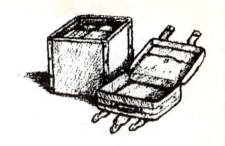

CHAPTER TWO

Charlie walked into the front room carefully carrying the big, heavy cake tin. Simon tugged at Charlie's sleeve.

"Look, it moved!" he pointed at the cake tin.

"Shut up," hissed Charlie out of the corner of his mouth.

Mr Evans sat back against the cushions with a cup and saucer wobbling on top of his big belly. Mrs Evans sat on the edge of the sofa, sipping tea. "Oh, we do love this flat," she cooed. "It's so clean and friendly."

"Thank you, Charlie," said Mum, taking the cake tin and putting it on the coffee table.

"Mmm. Fairy cakes with white icing — my favourite," said Mr Evans, rattling the cup and saucer as he leaned forward.

From behind the sofa, Ben popped up. No one saw him grinning like a cat that had just caught a mouse.

"What a helpful son you have," said Mrs Evans to Mum, picking up the cake tin. "Is it alright if I help myself to . . . ?"

"AARRGHH!"

Mum screamed so loudly at the thing that jumped out of the cake tin that Mrs Evans dropped the tin and it landed on Mr Evans' bunion. Mr Evans' leg shot into the air and up went the cup and saucer, splashing tea on his big belly.

Then Mum, who was always ticking off Charlie for putting his feet on the furniture, leapt on to the sofa in her high heels. She was so busy hopping about she didn't notice Ben laughing behind her. He laughed so much he fell backwards and disappeared.

"What's going on?" asked Dad, rushing into the room.

"It's a mouse," said Simon, crouching on all fours, looking under the sofa, "I can see him winking at me."

"I thought it was white icing with a cherry on top," said Mr Evans, "I must have pinched its nose."

Charlie opened his eyes wide and asked his father, "Have we got mice, Dad?"

"Nonsense!" said Dad.

Charlie tugged at Dad's shirt. "Does that mean Mr and Mrs Evans won't want to buy our flat any more?"

Dad got very flustered. And when he got flustered he became very bossy.

"We've never had mice — ever!" he said. "Everyone keep still and I'll find out what it really is"

"There he is! There he is!" shouted Simon, jumping up, now pointing at the arm of the sofa.

Mum shrieked and leaned across Mrs Evans, knocking her hat over her eyes. Then she stamped on Dad's back in her spiky heels, jumped on to the rug and ran out of the room.

And there sat the mouse. White and furry with a pink cherry nose, two little beady eyes and calm as anything. Then Mrs Evans did a very strange thing. She held out her hand! Charlie was shocked. Ben, who had stopped laughing and popped up again from behind the sofa was shocked too. Weren't old people supposed to be scared of small, furry things?

The mouse twitched its whiskers, sniffed around Mrs Evans' fingers and crept along until it was sitting in the palm of her hand.

"Isn't he sweet!" she cried, tickling its head.

"His name's Felix," said Simon, stroking him along his back and down to his long, pink tail.

Ben suddenly looked very worried. Charlie looked even more worried.

"How did you know that?" asked Dad.

By now Mum had crept back into the room. She leaned bravely towards the creature in Mrs Evans' hand, and took a good, hard look. Then she turned suspiciously towards Charlie. "Isn't that Felix — your school mouse?" she asked.

Charlie and Ben pretended not to hear. Ben slipped behind the sofa and Charlie tried to tiptoe backwards towards the

door. But Dad got there first.

"What's going on?" he asked.

Charlie looked up into his father's eyes and tried a winning smile.

"Miss asked me to look after him for the weekend," he said. Suddenly the smile turned into the most enormous burp. Charlie always did that when he was nervous.

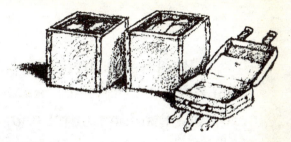

CHAPTER THREE

Charlie was in the hall looking through the letterbox. Ben was in the front room looking out of the window. Mum and Dad were upstairs putting labels on everything. Then it happened. Ben saw them first, but Charlie was the one to open the door before they rang the bell.

"You were quick off the mark!" said the first removal man who was tall and thin with a black moustache.

"We've come to move your furniture" said the second removal man who was broad and short and wearing a cap.

"I think you've got the wrong address," said Charlie.

"Bye!" said Ben, pushing the door shut.

But the door didn't budge because the short removal man had his big brown boot against it.

"It says here, number 59" he bellowed, looking at his clipboard.

"Ssshhh!" hushed Ben, hearing Mum and Dad moving about upstairs.

"Ssshhh," hushed Charlie.

"Perhaps we could speak to your parents," the tall, thin removal man whispered.

"They've gone out," Charlie whispered back, "and we're not allowed to open the door to strangers."

"Anyway, you've got the wrong address, so you'd better go," said Ben.

"Looks like we've got the wrong address," said the short removal man, as though he hadn't heard Ben say exactly the same thing.

"Any idea who is moving in this block?" asked the thin removal man. Charlie and Ben suddenly froze. They heard a noise behind them.

"Charlie" called Mum, coming down the stairs.

"Try 62" Ben shouted over Mum's voice. At the same time, Charlie kicked the door shut — just as Mum appeared in the hall.

"What were you shouting?" she asked. "I thought I heard someone."

"You did," said Charlie, truthfully. "It was Ben."

Mum gave Charlie one of her tired looks and said, "Well, call me as soon as you hear the removal men."

"We will," smiled Ben.

CHAPTER FOUR

Dad was on the phone — again. He tapped his feet impatiently as the phone on the other end rang and rang.

Charlie and Ben sat quietly around the table with two glasses of milk and two plates of biscuits in front of them.

"Still no answer!" said Dad, slamming down the phone.

"They're nearly an hour late!" sighed Mum, pacing around the kitchen. Ben snorted into his hands. Charlie suddenly felt the giggles coming on. He gulped some milk to stop himself and made laughter bubbles froth around his mouth.

"What's so funny?" snapped Dad,

"And why are you eating two plates of biscuits?"

Charlie stopped frothing into his milk. "One's for Ben," he said.

Dad made an irritated noise and Mum pointed her finger. "When we move into our new house I don't want you to ever mention that boy's name again!" she huffed.

Ben scowled at Mum and Dad. They always picked on him when things weren't going their way.

"Come on," said Mum. "Let's do something useful — see if we've forgotten to pack anything upstairs. Charlie, you too."

"I haven't forgotten anything," said Charlie, patting his bulging pockets. One was filled with a bag of marbles and the other with the last of his flour bombs. "Well, make yourself useful and go and look out for the removal men," grunted Dad as Mum led him up the stairs.

Charlie and Ben made their way on to the balcony. Ben leaned over and peered down into the courtyard.

"Bet you can't bomb the top of that van," he said.

"Bet I could," said Charlie, taking a flour bomb out of his pocket. He held it in the air, took aim, then stopped himself. "That's the removal van," he said.

"So?" said Ben.

"Why's it still here? There's no one in at Number 62. They're on holiday."

"Maybe those two men are waiting outside. They'll have a long wait," grinned Ben.

"Let's go and see," said Charlie.

Charlie and Ben leapt down two flights of stairs until they came to the fourth floor. Then they edged their way along the wall and carefully peeped round the corner.

"There's no one there," said Ben.

"Shhh!" hushed Charlie, tiptoeing along the balcony. When he was outside number 62, he held his breath and pointed for Ben to look. The door was slightly open and halfway up it was splintered

where the lock had been broken.

"Duck!" Ben suddenly cried, pulling Charlie to the ground.

"What?" asked Charlie.

"Careful," whispered Ben as he raised himself slowly. They craned their necks beneath the window till their heads bobbed just above the ledge. There inside number 62 were the two removal men. The tall, thin one carefully held a crystal vase up to the light.

"What do you reckon this is worth?" he asked.

"Enough," said the short one, coming out of the kitchen with a silver teapot,

"Come on, we've been here long enough."

"We haven't done upstairs yet," said the thin one, stuffing the vase into a large black bag.

"Okay," said the fat removal man. "But we've gotta be quick. We've got those two in the back of the van to worry about."

"They won't be going anywhere," chuckled the other removal man. "Not the way we tied them up!"

The two men burst out laughing and stomped up the stairs in their heavy boots.

Charlie turned to Ben. "What are we going to do?"

"Run!" said Ben.

"We can't do that. We've got to call the

police," said Charlie.

"So your Mum and Dad can find out what we did? No way!" said Ben.

"But they'll steal everything!" said Charlie. "And it will be all our fault."

"It *is* all our fault!" said Ben. "I'm going." And he turned and headed for the stairs, expecting Charlie to follow.

But Charlie didn't care what Ben wanted to do. He thought for a few minutes then carefully pushed open the door. He knew Number 62 kept their phone just inside the hall.

Charlie had just dialled 999 when Ben crept inside. "Don't tell them who you are!" he said, tugging at Charlie's sleeve.

But Charlie knew exactly what to say. He put on a high, shaky voice, the sort his Mum used when she was worried.

"Police, please come to Cooper court . . . Number 62 . . . we're being robbed . . .

please hurry!"

Charlie slammed the phone down. His heart was thumping so hard it was lifting his T-shirt.

"Let's go!" he said.

"Not yet!" said Ben, creeping up the stairs with Charlie's bag of marbles. He'd slipped them out of Charlie's pocket when he was on the phone.

"What are you *doing*?" hissed Charlie.

"Making sure they have a nice trip," grinned Ben, laying a few marbles on every other step.

Charlie could now hear his heart beating in his ears. He ran over to help so Ben would hurry up and they could get out quickly. But before they reached the bottom the bedroom door flew open and

40

they heard the removal men stomping along the landing.

"Come on, let's get out of here," said one.

Charlie and Ben scrambled downstairs so fast, their feet flew over the last few steps and hit the landing with a bump.

"Hey, hold on!" they heard one of the men say as they crouched, trembling at the bottom, behind the stairs.

"What?" growled the other man.

"Someone's left marbles on the stairs."

"Who'd do that?"

"I dunno, but we're gonna find out . . . Careful how you go."

The stairs creaked above Charlie and Ben's heads as the men carefully made their way down. Ben tugged at Charlie to make a dash for the door. They both leapt to their feet, but halfway across the hall, Charlie's legs forgot how to run.

"It's them!" shouted the fat robber, pointing a finger at Charlie.

Charlie turned to look at the robbers. His legs were frozen to the spot. He saw them stomping down the stairs towards him, but he couldn't move.

"Run!" shouted Ben, at the door.

Just then, Charlie dug into his pockets, pulled out a handful of bombs, took aim and pelted as hard as he could. The first bomb sailed over the robbers' heads. The second hit the fat man full in the face, exploding into a white cloud.

"Urghhh!" he cried, stumbling forwards, then backwards.

The thin removal man behind him stepped on a marble. His legs went up and he thudded against his partner. The black bag fell out of his hand and made a racket as it crashed down the stairs. Then the two robbers followed, skidding and tripping and tumbling towards Charlie and Ben.

"Come on!" shouted Ben, dragging Charlie by the arm.

Just as they slammed the door they could hear the police car wailing as it pulled into the courtyard.

CHAPTER FIVE

Mum had packed away all Charlie's clothes, so the wardrobe was the perfect place for Charlie and Ben to hide

"Charlie! Charlie!"

They could hear Mum and Dad calling around the house.

Charlie was glad he wasn't alone. The wardrobe was dark and spooky and they'd been hiding for ages. Suddenly, they heard a 'creak!' Charlie and Ben shuffled close to one another. Then there was another 'creak!' and a bit of light fell on Charlie's chest. Someone was opening the door! But who? It couldn't be Mum or Dad, because Charlie and Ben could hear

them calling out downstairs.

Suddenly everything was bright and Charlie and Ben had to blink like windscreen wipers so they could see properly. Then the blur cleared and something dark with little shiny round bits moved in front of them.

"Well, well, well!" said the policeman.

Charlie and Ben could now see very clearly that they were in big trouble.

"Not very clever hiding in wardrobes," said the policeman, "Don't you realise you could suffocate in there?"

But all Charlie could think of was his prison sentence — the one he'd get for sending burglars to rob his neighbours' flat. He cupped his hand over his mouth, but it was too late to stop it.

"Burp!"

Mum and Dad ran into Charlie's room.

"There you are!" said Dad.

"What have you been up to?" asked Mum. But before Charlie could say anything, she said crossly, "And don't you dare say it was Ben!"

"I've heard quite a bit about this Ben," said the policeman.

"He told me to do everything," blurted Charlie. "He's the one who doesn't want to move."

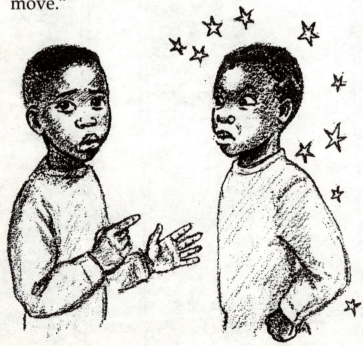

Ben gave Charlie a filthy look, but Charlie was only telling the truth — for once. The policeman walked slowly around the room. "Once your removal men — your real removal men — have finished helping with our enquiries, I expect you'll be ready to start moving."

Charlie and Ben said nothing.

The policeman stopped at Charlie's suitcase.

"Is this big enough for both your clothes?" he asked.

Charlie nodded.

"I'm talking to Ben," said the policeman.

Mum and Dad looked around the room. They couldn't see Ben anywhere.

"If Ben doesn't pack his belongings now, in front of all the witnesses in this room, I'm afraid I'll have to take you both down to the police station for questioning," said the policeman.

It was the first time Charlie had seen Ben move so quickly. The policeman watched as Ben dashed around the room picking up his clothes, toys and belongings and putting them in the suitcase. Mum and Dad watched even though they weren't sure what they were meant to be watching. Soon the suitcase was filled to the top.

"And don't think that's the end of it," said the policeman. "I'll be visiting your new house to see that you're both behaving yourselves. Is that clear?"

"Yes, sir," said Ben, thoroughly ashamed of himself.

"Yes, sir," said Charlie.

And with that, the policeman left the room. Two seconds later the door inched open and his helmet poked into the room.

"One more thing," he said. "Thanks

for helping me and my officers catch those crooks. Don't know what we'd do without neighbours like you two." And then he was gone.

Charlie and Ben looked at each other. But this time Charlie swallowed the burp.

CHAPTER SIX

Charlie and Ben looked out of the back window and watched the block of flats get smaller and smaller as the car followed the removal van. Then they turned the corner and the flats disappeared altogether. They passed the adventure playground, the chip shop, the launderette and the pub on the corner. They passed the street where Charlie's teacher lived and his old nursery up the road and all the streets and roads he knew. Then everything changed. The houses, roads and shops were all strange and different.

Charlie and Ben turned to the front of the car and became very quiet. Even Mum and Dad were quiet. Outside, the roads now had trees on every corner and the pavements had patches of grass where children were playing ball or riding bicycles and the houses had little gardens in front. Dad stopped the car when the removal van pulled up outside a house with a white front door and a green hedge. A group of children gathered around to watch.

"Come on, Charlie," said Mum. "Aren't you getting out?"

Charlie wanted to stay inside the car and sulk with Ben, but he remembered what the policeman said so he got out.

Mum and Dad pointed to the house.

"See how big it is?" said Mum.

"And look how many children there are for you to play with," said Dad.

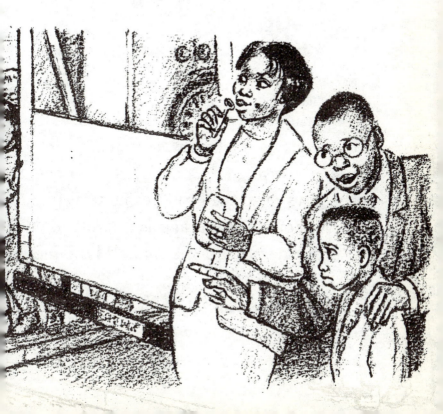

Charlie looked at Ben in the car. He was pressing his grumpy face against the window, refusing to get out. Just then one of the boys from the group came forward. He was about the same age as Charlie.

"I live next door," he said. "My name is Jack."

"We'll leave you to chat, Charlie," said

Mum. "Dad and I will start unpacking."

When Mum and Dad disappeared into the house, Jack and the crowd shuffled closer.

"Mark, Sabrina, Roger, Neela, Tom, Daniel and Margaret," said Jack, calling out his friends' names.

"What about me?" said a tiny voice.

A little girl carrying a piece of string pushed her way through the crowd.

"Oh, . . . and that's my sister, Katy," said Jack. Then he pulled Charlie to one

side and whispered in his ear. "But she's weird."

"I'm not weird!" shouted Katy stamping her feet.

"Guess what's on the end of that string," said Jack to Charlie.

The crowd started laughing and pointing at Katy's string.

"His name's Fozzy," said Katy. "And he's my dog."

Jack and the crowd laughed again.

"See what I mean," he said.

Charlie couldn't see the dog, but he couldn't see what was so funny either.

"Let's go up the Rec!" someone shouted.

"Yeah!" everyone cried.

"Can Fozzy come?" asked Katy.

"Woof! Woof!" laughed Jack, running off with the others, making fun. "Come on, Charlie!" he called.

"Woof! Woof!" said someone else. Charlie turned round. Ben had got out of the car. He came over and patted Fozzy on the head.

"Who's he?" Katy asked Charlie.

"My friend Ben," said Charlie.

"Come on, Katy," said Ben, taking hold of the string. "Let's take Fozzy for a walk."

Charlie watched Ben and Katy walk up the road together. It was the first time Ben had gone off with someone else. But somehow it didn't matter. Charlie turned and ran to catch up with the others.

"Wait for me!" he cried.

No, it didn't matter at all.

Other brilliant Orchard Books are:

THE SCRIBBLERS OF SCUMBAGG SCHOOL
Wes Magee
ISBN 1 85213 486 0 HB
ISBN 1 85213 510 7 PB

THE WITCH WHO COULDN'T SPELL
Jonathan Allen
ISBN 1 85213 887 4 HB

TEACHER'S PET
Philip Wooderson
ISBN 1 85213 977 3 HB

GALACTACUS THE AWESOME
Andrew Matthews
ISBN 1 85213 780 0 HB